PHANTOM
TRUCKER

by Jason K. Friedman

BULLSEYE CHILLERS™
Random House 🏠 New York

For Tim

A BULLSEYE BOOK PUBLISHED BY RANDOM HOUSE, INC.

Text copyright © 1996 by Jason K. Friedman.
Cover art copyright © 1996 by Jeff Walker.

http://www.randomhouse.com/
Library of Congress Cataloging-in-Publication Data:
Friedman, Jason.
    Phantom trucker / by Jason K. Friedman.
        p. cm. — (Bullseye chillers)
    "A Bullseye book" — T.p. verso.
    Summary: C. J. Bulloch grows up steeped in the legends his father tells
when he comes home after a long day behind the wheel, but the tale of a
ghost trucker is more than C.J. can handle.
    ISBN 0-679-87437-2
    [1. Truck drivers—Fiction. 2. Ghosts—Fiction. 3. Fathers and sons—
Fiction.] I. Title II. Series.
PZ7.F8978Ph 1996 [Fic]—dc20 95-32564

Printed in the United States of America 10 9 8 7 6 5 4 3 2 1

CONTENTS

CHAPTER 1

River Giants

One hot summer evening, C.J. Bulloch and his little sister, Lulu, were sitting in the kitchen of their family's pink cottage. C.J. was telling Lulu scary stories. Suddenly they heard their father's voice. It was coming from the little gray box on the counter.

"KKN 0712, mobile to base, this is Big Daddy calling the Little Darlings. Come in, please." Big Daddy was the name, or "handle," their father used on the CB radio. C.J. and Lulu shared the handle "Little Darlings."

Their mother, who was in the living room watching TV, used the handle "Big Mama."

C.J. and Lulu jumped up at the same time. The box was attached to a microphone by a curly black cord. They both tried to grab the microphone. But C.J., who was almost twelve, got it first.

"We read you, Big Daddy!" he shouted into the microphone. Their father's voice sounded very close. But C.J. knew he was probably in a different state. Lee Bulloch was a short-haul trucker. He drove an eighteen-wheeler. He delivered big containers of Park's ice cream to stores all over the Southeast.

"I just passed by Ridgeland, South Carolina," Big Daddy said. The Bullochs' cottage was in a clearing in the woods just outside Savannah, Georgia. Their father was about thirty miles away. "I'll be home in just over half an hour."

"We're hungry," C.J. said.

"So am I," their father said. "I'll pick up a bucket of chicken on the way home. But y'all better have that table set."

Lulu grabbed the microphone. "Don't

forget the slaw!"

"Ten-four," said Big Daddy's voice over the CB. "Tell Big Mama I'm on the way. This is Big Daddy, over and out."

C.J. went into the living room. His mother was watching *America's Funniest Home Videos*. Her pink curlers and purple house-dress glowed in the TV's blue light. "Dad's on his way home," he told her.

"Did you see that?" she said, still looking at the TV screen. "That lady's pet pig is smarter than me!"

C.J. laughed. His mother always zoned out when she watched TV.

He went back to the kitchen. Lulu was singing some dumb song. She went to the cupboard and took out four plates with Barney on them. She put the plates on the table. Then she went to the refrigerator and got the ketchup.

C.J. stood at the sink and watched the sun go down behind the pine trees. The sky went from orange to red, the color of blood. Because of his job, C.J.'s dad often didn't get home until nighttime.

Lulu came up behind him and said,

"You're supposed to be helping me!"

Little sisters are such a pain sometimes, C.J. thought as he stared out the window at the backyard. On the other side of the yard, trees grew out of a bluff rising from a shallow creek.

C.J. knew Lulu was afraid of the creek. Roots and trunks of cypress trees stuck out from the water. C.J. and Lulu's parents called these brown growths "knees." Lulu thought they were real knees. She thought "river giants" lay with their backs against the creek bed and their knees sticking up.

C.J. turned around and said, "I think I saw a river giant."

Lulu, who was getting some forks, suddenly froze.

"He's big and ugly and covered with green slime," C.J. went on.

Lulu still didn't move. She seemed to be holding her breath.

"He's gonna grab you with his slimy hands and choke you till you're dead," C.J. said.

Slowly Lulu made her way to the table. She put down the forks next to the plates.

Then, without looking at her brother, she said, "Mama said there's no such thing as a river giant."

"What? She never said that."

Lulu turned around. "Yes, she did, you liar. She said there's no such thing as a river giant."

"Well, why would she say that?" C.J. asked. "Everyone knows they're real. Who else do you think all those big knobby knees belong to?"

Lulu took a second to think that over. Then she walked to the sink and pushed C.J. out of the way. She stood on tiptoe, but she was too short to see out the window. "Lift me up," she commanded.

C.J. laughed to himself and picked her up. Outside, the light was fading. Suddenly Lulu screamed and jumped out of her brother's arms.

"River giant's coming!" she shouted, running out of the kitchen. "Coming to get us!"

C.J. kept looking out the window. It really did look as if something was moving among the trees. Were those "knees" bending? What if a giant really did sleep on the creek bed? What if he was getting up to find something—or *someone*—to eat?

Chill out, he told himself. *You're losing it.* It was probably just a trick of the dying light. There wasn't anything or anyone out there.

Now Lulu was running around the house turning on every light and screaming. At first C.J. thought this was hilarious. Then he started to feel bad about teasing his sister. After all, she was only eight.

"Hey, y'all be quiet!" their mother shouted from the living room. "I can't hear my show."

Lulu ran back into the kitchen, still screaming, "River giant's coming!" She turned on the light over the kitchen table. Then she yanked the curtains closed.

"There's no such thing as a river giant," said C.J. "I was just kidding you."

Lulu ran to the back screen door and latched it. Then she slammed the back door shut. C.J. grabbed her and told her to stop acting crazy.

"I saw him!" she said, pulling away from

C.J. "I did! He was coming up here. Coming to get us." She ran screaming to her room.

C.J. pulled the curtains aside and peeked out. It was almost completely dark outside. The kitchen lights were reflected in the window.

C.J. went to check on Lulu. She was lying in her bed with a pillow over her head. Strands of blond hair escaped from under her pillow, like tentacles. "You're going to suffocate that way," he told her.

"I don't care," Lulu said. "At least *he* won't be able to get me."

"How do you figure that?" C.J. asked.

"Well, if I can't see him, then maybe he can't see me."

All of a sudden someone kicked open the front door!

CHAPTER 2

Horror for Supper

"I'm home!"

C.J. peeked out of Lulu's room. Their father was standing in the doorway. He was a tall man with a big smile on his sun-burned face. He had a bucket of chicken in one hand and a box of rolls and coleslaw in the other.

Lulu was still hiding her head under the pillow. C.J. pulled the pillow off and said, "It's just Dad, you scaredy-cat." Then he ran to the front door.

"Hey there, Little Darling," Lee Bulloch said. He handed C.J. the bucket of chicken. Then he put his Park's ice cream cap on C.J.'s curly blond head.

"Hey, Dad," C.J. said.

"Let's eat!" their mother called from the kitchen. "I'm starved!"

"Me too," Lulu said. She raced to the door. Lee handed her the box he was holding. "Thanks, Daddy!" she said.

"Any time." Their father looked around. "Hey, kids, this place is lit up like a Christmas tree. I could see it from the road."

Lulu looked at C.J. He knew she didn't want him to tell their father how crazy she'd been acting. *Okay,* he thought, *I won't tell. But only if she doesn't bug me.*

At the table they scarfed down the food.

"This is delicious," said Rhonda Bulloch, sucking chicken grease off her pinkie. "You kids sure are lucky to have such a good daddy. Works hard all day and then brings home supper to boot."

"Well, I don't know about that," Lee said, shrugging. But he looked secretly pleased.

"No, it's true." Rhonda reached for her

9

third roll. "Tell us all about your day and we'll tell you about ours."

C.J. rolled his eyes. Last month Oprah had done a show about happy families who talk a lot at the dinner table. After she saw that show, Rhonda wouldn't allow TV at supper. During supper, the little black-and-white TV, which sat on the counter next to the CB radio, was dark. And she forced them to make polite conversation when they would all rather just eat.

"I'll tell you about my day," Lulu said.

"Go ahead, sweetheart," Lee said.

"Well…first, I got up and ate breakfast," Lulu began. She was talking slowly and seriously. "You were already gone by then, Daddy. I had pancakes. They had pecans in them. They were yummy! Then…I went out to the backyard. I thought it was going to rain. I didn't want the ants to get wet. I got a big leaf and put it on top of the anthill. Then…I went inside and watched TV with Mama. We saw—"

If he had to listen to another word of his sister's boring story, C.J. was going to scream. He liked to spend the summer outdoors, exploring the woods. He liked plants and bugs. But sometimes he wished his life was more exciting. He wished something would happen!

Lulu was talking about her life as if it was the most exciting thing in the world. She was probably doing it to bother him, to get back at him for teasing her about river giants. And she wasn't going to shut up any time soon.

Before C.J. knew it, the words were out of his mouth: "And things really got fun when she started running around the house turning on all the lights like a crazy person!"

Lulu turned to him. Her face was red. C.J. immediately felt bad for what he'd said. He didn't know what got into him sometimes.

"Well, that's because you were scaring me so bad!" she shot back.

"I was just teasing," he said.

"Were not!" Lulu said. "You said there was a river giant outside."

"Honestly, C.J.," his mother said, "you should be ashamed of yourself."

"Yeah," Lulu agreed, and stuck out her tongue at her brother.

"Now, kids, y'all stop that," said their

father. "There's no such thing as a river giant, and that's that."

"That's right," Rhonda said, her mouth full of chicken.

"Besides," Lee said, "I bet Lulu was brave compared to the folks at the truck stop this afternoon."

"What happened?" C.J. asked. He stuck his hand in the bucket, looking for another drumstick.

"Well, I was having a cup of coffee with some of the other drivers," Lee said. "We were sitting in the truckers-only section of Ma's Truck Stop. You know, the place I like to stop at just north of Manning, South Carolina. And a lady mentioned she spotted our old friend Warren Cleary out on the highway. Everyone was shaking in their boots."

C.J. noticed his mom shoot his dad a worried look.

"Who's Warren Cleary?" C.J. asked.

"Never mind," Rhonda said. "Hey, who wants more slaw? I think this is about the best slaw I ever ate."

C.J. knew his mom didn't want his dad

to tell about Warren Cleary. That made C.J. want to hear about him even more!

"Yeah, who's Warren Clearly?" Lulu asked.

"Cleary!" C.J. corrected her.

"He's no one," their father said. "Just another driver I used to work with."

C.J. could tell his parents were hiding something. Who was Warren Cleary? And why didn't their folks want him and Lulu to hear about the guy?

C.J. looked at his dad and then at his mom. He could see his dad really wanted to tell. Mama was just no fun sometimes! So C.J. said to his father, "Why don't you work with Warren Cleary anymore?"

"Well," Lee said, "I just don't."

"Yeah," Lulu said, "why not? What happened to him, Daddy? Come on, tell us! Tell us!"

"See what you've done now?" Rhonda stood up. "They don't need to be stirred up with more scary stories, especially ones that aren't even true."

"Honey," Lee said, "kids love a good story. Nothing wrong with that."

C.J. loved scary stories the best. Now he knew he had to find out all about Warren Cleary. But Lulu looked as if she was already starting to get scared. C.J. decided to wait until he was alone with his father to ask about Warren Cleary again. He'd give Lulu a break. He'd already freaked her out enough for one day.

But it was Lulu who said, in a trembling voice, "What did he do that was so scary?"

Rhonda went over to the kitchen sink and stared out the window. Her arms were crossed over her chest. She chewed on her lower lip. She always did that when she was really worried.

Lee glanced over at her. Then he turned back to the kids. "Since I already let the cat out of the bag, I might as well tell you about our old friend Warren. Now, this is just a story. It's not real. But a lot of folks would disagree with me. A lot of people—like that lady driver at the truck stop today—see him driving up and down I-95 in the same Park's ice cream truck he used to drive. Driving a big rig just like every other trucker heading up and down the highway."

14

Their father paused. Lulu's eyes were bugging out.

"There's just one difference." Lee took a deep breath. "He's dead."

CHAPTER 3

The Phantom Trucker

"They call him the Phantom Trucker," Lee said. "Do y'all know what that means?"

"Does that mean he's ugly?" Lulu asked.

"No," C.J. said. "A phantom's a ghost."

"That's right," Lee said. "Folks say he's a ghost."

"But I thought there's no such thing as ghosts," Lulu said.

"That's right, sugar," Rhonda said, turning back to the table. "There's no such thing. Excuse me for saying so, Lee, but it

16

seems to me some of those drivers have gone off the deep end."

C.J. laughed. His mother was kind of flaky herself. But he had to agree with her. Anyone who saw ghosts had a major problem.

"It's a stressful job, honey," Lee explained. "Driving all hours of the day and night, not getting enough sleep."

"So maybe they're just seeing things," she said.

"I don't know," Lee said. "When that lady driver at the truck stop said she saw Warren, everyone else nodded their heads. They had all seen him too, at one time or another. I guess he's pretty famous around Ma's."

"Did you ever see him, Daddy?" C.J. asked.

"Well, like I said, son, I used to work with him. But I can't say I ever saw him after the accident."

"How about some dessert, kids?" Rhonda said, ignoring Lee. She came back to the table and started gathering the empty boxes and greasy plates. "I've got

17

some of that delicious chocolate dream pie left over. Who wants some with Cool Whip?"

"What accident?" C.J. asked.

"Yeah," Lulu said. "What accident?"

"Never mind." Lee looked up at Rhonda. "I'll have a teensy piece of pie."

"No way, Daddy," C.J. said. "Finish what you started. That's what you're always telling me."

"Yeah," Lulu said. "Start what you finished."

C.J. gave his sister a look. What a ditz!

Rhonda gave Lee a different kind of look.

Lee shrugged and said, "All right, all right. I see I have no choice but to tell y'all about Warren Cleary."

Their mother sat down at the table and folded her hands. She didn't look happy.

"Warren was a nice guy. Kind of quiet, kept to himself. Your mama never met him, but he and I always said hello when we ran into each other at the plant. He had a headful of bushy red hair. Anyway, one night— this was two or three years ago—he had just delivered a big load to a supermarket up in

Sumter, South Carolina. His truck was empty. He wanted to get home fast. But first he needed a cup of coffee for the road. He was tired and didn't want to fall asleep at the wheel. So he turned off into the first truck stop he saw. You kids have probably guessed by now that it was Ma's Truck Stop. The parking lot was full, so he drove around looking for a space.

"Anyway, as he drove past the restaurant part of the truck stop, a boy—I guess he was about your age, C.J.—noticed Warren's rig. It looked just like the one I drive. It had big, bright ice cream cones painted on the side of the trailer. So that kid must have snuck away from his folks and gone outside. He wanted to see the ice cream truck.

"Just then, poor old Warren yawned. Remember, he was tuckered out, and he hadn't gotten his cup of coffee yet. So, he yawned—and when he opened his eyes, that boy was right in front of him!"

Lulu was shaking. Her eyes were wide open.

"I've heard enough," said Rhonda.

"Did the boy get killed?" C.J. asked. He

19

couldn't help himself.

"No," Lee said, "he didn't. Warren swerved out of the way in the nick of time. Unfortunately, he ran right smack into a light pole at the edge of the parking lot. The pole smashed into his windshield. Killed him. People say his ghost has got a bloody gash running all the way down its face."

Lulu screamed and ran from the room.

Rhonda went after her.

C.J. felt his heart beating fast. He hoped his father couldn't tell.

Lee leaned over to him. "How'd you like to come with me to the plant tomorrow? See what goes on there. Your sister's still too young, but one day I'll take her there, too. Once you get to know how the trucking industry works, you'll be able to laugh at these silly old stories."

"I'm not scared," C.J. said. He hoped he sounded as if he meant it!

"I know you're not," Lee said. "Now, how about it? Want to go in with me tomorrow? I'll take care of my paperwork and take you on a tour."

"Sure, Daddy," C.J. said. "That sounds cool."

*   *   *

That night C.J. couldn't sleep. He was very excited about going to the Park's ice cream plant tomorrow. He thought about becoming a trucker one day, too.

Suddenly he heard something outside. It was the sound of tree branches breaking.

Then the night was quiet. It had been a cloudy day. A storm was probably coming.

But C.J. heard the sound again. He got out of bed and looked out the window. Outside his window was a tall wooden pole. The pole had a faint light and two antennas on top—one for the CB radio, the other for the TV.

C.J. looked up. There was a full yellow moon—and not one cloud was in the sky.

It wasn't going to storm. There was something out there. But the woods were full of animals. C.J. had probably heard a big raccoon or a deer.

Or could the noise be coming from something else?

Now C.J. was hearing different sounds. Sloshing water. And grass and underbrush being trampled.

Something was coming out of the creek.

21

Heading up the bluff. Crossing the yard.

C.J. could feel his heart beating in his ears.

Suddenly a tall figure stumbled into the dim light. It looked like a man. He was over six feet tall. Swamp weeds hung off his clothes. He had a dark bandanna tied around his neck. His face was hidden under a cap.

This can't be happening, C.J. thought. *River giants aren't real.*

But the figure was heading straight for the back door of the cottage!

C.J. grabbed his baseball bat and ran to the back door. He heard the screen door swing open. Then the door itself flew off its hinges and crashed open!

C.J. jumped out of the way and found himself face to face with the intruder. The man's face was split in half by a deep, bloody gash. Messy red hair curled from under his cap, which said PARK'S.

It wasn't a river giant. It was Warren Cleary!

22

CHAPTER 4

Slipping and Sliding

"Aaaaaahhhhh!"

Someone was shaking him. "You were having a bad dream," Lulu said.

C.J. opened one eye. There was his little sister, standing over him and grinning.

Great, he thought. *Now I'll never be able to tease her again.* But that didn't mean he was going to let *her* start teasing *him.*

"What were you dreaming about?" Lulu asked.

"I wasn't dreaming about anything." C.J. sat up.

"Were too."

"Was not. Now get out of here. I've got to get ready to go with Daddy to the factory."

"I'm going over to Susan's house," Lulu said, and ran out of the room.

When he was ready to go, C.J. said good-bye to his mom. She was sitting at the kitchen table eating Park's butter pecan ice cream and watching a game show.

"See you, sweetie," she said, holding the spoon up and staring at the screen.

C.J. figured he could be kidnapped or something and, if it happened during her favorite TV shows, his mother would never notice.

C.J.'s father was out front. His head was under the hood of his pickup truck.

"All set?" he asked, straightening up, when C.J. came out.

"Yeah," C.J. replied, yawning. That dream had seemed so real. "Let's roll."

C.J. stood in front of the long window above the squeaky-clean assembly-line floor. Below him mechanical arms stirred enormous vats of ice cream. On another part of the floor, boxes of ice cream shuttled down a white conveyor belt. No people worked down there. It was too cold.

Earlier Lee had taken him to the yard, where dozens of eighteen-wheelers were parked in rows. Every truck had the same three flavors of ice cream cone painted on its sides. The trucks all looked alike to C.J. But Lee had told him that every rig had its own name and its own personality.

They had even gone inside one of the trucks. C.J.'s father had shown him everything.

An eighteen-wheeler basically had two parts. The tractor—which contained the front-seat area, known as the "cab"—pulled the semi-trailer, which was a huge cargo container. The driver sat so high that he had to climb into the cab on a ladder attached to the side of the truck. The cab had a gigantic gearshift with twenty gears. The truck's control panel looked as complicated as an airplane's.

Now C.J. was waiting for his father to come back from the office to give him a tour of the factory. It was going to be really cool. But first his father had to turn in his logbook. In the logbook Lee recorded how many miles he traveled on his trips, how much diesel fuel he used, and how long he took getting there and back. The logbook also showed the weigh-station results. At the weigh station, his dad had told him, trucks drove up on a giant scale.

C.J. felt a hand on his neck. Well, it was about time his dad got done with his boring paperwork.

C.J. turned around. But instead of his father smiling, it was Warren Cleary leering down at him! His eyes were bloodshot. And his face looked as if it had been gashed just five minutes ago! The wound was dripping with blood.

This can't be happening, C.J. thought, holding back a scream. *I must be dreaming.*

But suddenly C.J. felt excruciating pain. Warren had him in a choke hold!

C.J. kicked him in the shin. Warren cried out. His grip loosened for a second.

C.J. tore off. At the end of the hall was a door with a red sign: TO PLANT FLOOR: EMPLOYEES ONLY.

I hope I count as an employee, C.J. thought, *because I'm sure going through that door.*

Behind him he could hear Warren's heavy boots pounding the floor in pursuit.

C.J. pushed open the door. He stumbled down a cement stairway. At the bottom he looked up. Warren was already halfway down!

C.J. burst through the door at the bottom of the stairs. The cold hit him like a fist. He was standing on the shiny white floor. There was a door on the other side of the factory floor, far in the distance. But an obstacle course of gleaming stainless-steel ice cream vats stood in his way.

Behind him the door flew open.

C.J. sprinted behind one of the vats. He listened for Warren but couldn't hear anything over the sound of ice cream churning. He peered over the edge of the vat.

There was no sign of Warren Cleary.

C.J. noticed his breath puffing out like a cloud. He might give himself away just by breathing. He held his breath as long as he could. His hands and ears were numb.

Finally he decided to make his move.

Seven ice cream vats stretched in a row to the exit. If he ran straight past them he might be able to make it.

He sucked air and took off. He passed one vat, then another. He saw the exit in the distance. He couldn't see Warren anywhere.

C.J. zipped past a third vat, then a fourth.

Three more to go! C.J.'s head felt as if it was going to split open. His lungs burned.

Suddenly the next vat started to move. Warren was tipping it over!

C.J. tried to change course but started to slide on the polished tiles. With a terrible crash the vat tipped over. Mushy strawberry ice cream flooded the floor.

C.J. landed right in the middle of it.

Warren appeared from behind the vat and reached down to grab him!

Ice Cream Man

As C.J. scrambled to get up, the door swung open and Lee ran in.

"Watch out!" C.J. shouted at his father.

"What's going on here?" Lee said, stopping at the edge of the giant pink ice cream puddle. C.J. was still trying to get to his feet.

"It's Warren Cleary," C.J. cried, gasping for breath. "He must be hiding behind one of those vats!"

"Are you all right?" his father asked.

C.J. finally got up and started to run. But

he slipped and fell again!

Lee's worried expression turned into a smile. "This is about the funniest thing I've ever seen," he said.

"We've got to get out of here!" C.J. shouted, crawling across the mess on all fours.

Lee was bent over in laughter. "How'd you know I was thinking about getting a cat?" he said. "You must be practicing for the job." He reached out to give C.J. a hand.

At the edge of the ice cream lake, C.J. stood up and threw himself at the door.

"Whoa!" Lee said, catching him.

"Come on!" C.J. said. "We need to get out of here! Now!"

"You're right about that. But take it easy. If you hadn't been running, you wouldn't have made that mess in the first place."

They went into the company washroom. Lee handed C.J. a stack of paper towels.

"I tell you, Dad," C.J. said, "Warren Cleary was after me."

"Park's is going to be after you now," Lee said. "Do you know how much money you just cost the company?"

C.J. couldn't believe what he was hearing. He'd almost gotten killed, and his dad was on his case for making a mess!

"You don't believe me," C.J. said.

"I didn't say that," Lee said. "You're still shivering. Splash some warm water on your face."

"He's not really dead, Dad. He's *un*dead. And he's somewhere in this factory."

"All right, suppose he is, as you put it, undead," Lee answered. "What would he be doing chasing you?"

"How should I know?" C.J. crumpled the last of the paper towels and threw it away. "Hey, wait a minute. Didn't you say that kid who ran out in front of his rig was about my age?"

"Yeah."

"Then what if he thinks I'm the one who did it?" C.J. asked. "What if he's trying to get revenge?"

His father got the weirdest expression C.J. had ever seen. It was stronger than worry—it was fear.

"What is it, Dad?"

"Oh, it's nothing."

"Come on, Dad. Spit it out."

"All right," Lee said. "But I'm just repeating what that lady at the truck stop said yesterday. You know I don't believe in ghosts, right?"

"I know it," C.J. said. *He* didn't believe in ghosts, either. But Warren Cleary was no ordinary ghost.

"Okay, that lady said something like what you were just saying."

"She did?" C.J. felt frozen in place by the sink.

Lee nodded. "She said the reason Warren Cleary's still driving is to get revenge on that kid. Except he doesn't even remember what the boy looks like. So every boy about that age is fair game."

C.J. loved walking in the woods, with a smooth carpet of pine needles beneath his feet. Under the trees, it was dark and cool. It was also quiet and still. Sometimes he felt he could think straight only when he was out here.

His dad had gone to the Hardware Depot and his mom had been watching her soaps when C.J. got back from the factory. His mother didn't notice his soggy clothes and sticky hair. And Lulu was still at her friend's house. C.J. had stashed the dirty clothes in the back of his closet and cleaned himself up. Then he went for a walk. He needed to get out and think for a while.

He picked up a branch and broke it in two. Bluejays perched in the trees sang down at him.

Maybe his imagination was just running away with him. After all, those stories about Warren Cleary were scary! Last night C.J. had had a nightmare. Maybe today he was just having a daymare—and it seemed real.

Besides, Lulu was the family scaredy-cat, not him.

From the road he heard the Park's ice cream truck jingle. C.J. whistled the tune. Old Ben Smith drove the truck—C.J.'s father called it a shoebox on wheels—from neighborhood to neighborhood. There weren't many other houses out here, but Mr. Smith still came around from time to time. He liked to say, "I don't want even one kid to miss out on Park's delicious ice cream!"

The jingle was faint but growing louder. C.J.'s dad brought home tons of Park's ice cream, but there was still something fun about getting it from Mr. Smith. Seeing the old man's smiling face would make C.J. feel even better. And he could use a cold drink.

C.J. ran out to the road. The truck puttered toward him.

The Park's tune got louder.

Soon the truck was close enough for C.J. to make out Mr. Smith's cap.

C.J. walked out into the road. The truck slowed down and came to a stop.

C.J. went up to it and said, "Hi, Mr. Smith."

The driver had his head down and was jotting notes on a clipboard. Slowly he looked up.

It was Warren Cleary staring straight at C.J., inches from his face!

C.J. tore off down the dirt road. Behind him Warren Cleary floored the truck's accelerator.

C.J. turned his head and saw the truck gaining on him! The road dead-ended up ahead. C.J. leaped into the woods. Running through the trees, he realized he couldn't hear the truck anymore. He turned around, and there was Warren Cleary—chasing him on foot!

C.J. ran harder than he ever had before. He wasn't going to let Warren catch him. Out here his body might not be found for weeks!

Luckily, C.J. knew these woods well. He had to know them better than Warren Cleary did. He took a shortcut home. It was a path C.J. himself had made over the years. He charged down it without looking back. It was his only chance.

Behind him he could hear footsteps and heavy breathing growing louder.

C.J. could see sunlight up ahead. That meant he was coming back to the road. The path came out across the road from his house. If he could just make it to the road, he'd be safe!

Finally he broke out of the trees. He raced across the road, jumped over the ditch in front of the pink cottage, and—

And there was Lulu, walking across the

lawn, jangling a fistful of change.

"I heard the ice cream man," she said, skipping toward the road. "I hope I can still catch him."

"No!" C.J. shouted, running toward her. "Get back in the house!"

"What's your problem?" she asked, stopping in her tracks. "Daddy forgot to bring home fudge bars this time and I want one now."

"Get back in the house!" C.J. shouted. "Warren Cleary's right behind me!"

CHAPTER 6

Crazy

"I am *so* sure," Lulu said, rolling her eyes. She began skipping toward him again. Obviously, nothing was going to come between her and her fudge bar. C.J. had no choice but to tackle her, right on the lawn.

"Help!" Lulu shouted. "Help!"

As if C.J. was the bad guy here!

"Let me up or I'm going to tell Mama and Daddy!" Lulu said.

"Shhh." C.J. had Lulu pinned to the ground, but he kept looking back over his shoulder. "We've got to get back in the house."

Suddenly the Park's ice cream jingle started up. It was coming from the end of the dirt road. And getting louder.

C.J. raised himself a bit so he could see the truck. Lulu shot out from under him and ran to the ditch.

C.J. ran after her. Lulu jumped across the ditch.

The jingle was booming. The truck was heading down the dirt road toward C.J. And it was picking up speed.

The ice cream truck was heading toward them faster than any car C.J. had ever seen. He was afraid Lulu would run right in front of it if he ran after her, so he stood back.

Lulu held up her fistful of change and waved it at the truck.

The driver had his cap pulled down over his head, but C.J. knew it was Warren Cleary.

The truck sped past them in a cloud of red dust.

Lulu coughed and turned around. "You are *such* a dork," she said. "You scared Mr.

Smith away. Why did you have to act so weird?"

"It wasn't Mr. Smith." C.J. wiped his forehead with the back of his hand. "It was Warren Cleary, the Phantom Trucker!"

Lulu thought about this for a second. "But I thought he wasn't real," she said.

"Me too," C.J. said. "But he *is* real. Or else I'm going crazy."

"Is crazy the same as weird?" she asked.

"Very funny," C.J. said. "But when he gets me, you won't be laughing anymore."

"Don't be afraid," she said softly. "Daddy told me not to be afraid of river giants."

River giants aren't real, C.J. wanted to say. *Warren Cleary is.* But why should Lulu believe him?

"Come on," he said. "I'll walk you to the store and we can get you that fudge bar."

When they got back, their father's pickup truck was parked on the lawn. Inside, his new purchases were all spread out on the living room floor. On the TV screen a dark-haired woman was kissing a blond man. The sound was turned down low.

"That new Hardware Depot superstore is great," Lee was saying.

"Sure is," Rhonda agreed absently.

"Hey, look who's here," Lee said.

C.J. plopped down on the couch next to his mom.

"Hey, Daddy!" Lulu gave Lee a kiss. "Did you get anything for me?"

"How about a can of paint?" he asked.

"No way," she said. She picked up a plain white box and shook it. It rattled. "What's this?"

"Nails," he said. "Does my big girl want a box of nails?"

"Try again," she said.

Lee and Rhonda laughed. C.J. sat there and stared at the TV without really seeing it.

"What's the matter with you?" Rhonda asked C.J. "Cat got your tongue?"

"I'm fine," he said.

"Yeah, he's fine," Lulu agreed. "He's not going crazy or anything."

C.J. stared at his sister. She was unbelievable! At the store he'd made her promise not to say anything to their folks. He didn't want to worry them. But Lulu couldn't keep anything to herself.

"What's this about going crazy?" Lee asked. "I don't want anyone going crazy in this house."

"Nothing," C.J. said. "Lulu's just fooling around."

"Honey," Rhonda said, "if you don't mind my saying so, you're the one acting a little strange. And it's the middle of summer, but you're white as a ghost."

Thanks, Mama, C.J. thought. *That's really what I need to hear right now.*

"Are you still worrying about Warren Cleary?" Lee asked.

"Whatever," C.J. said.

"And guess what?" Lulu said, making herself comfortable on the floor.

"What?" Rhonda and Lee asked at the same time.

"Just now C.J. saw Warren Cleary driving Mr. Smith's truck!"

Lee got up and turned off the television.

"Hey, what did you do that for?" Rhonda asked. "Fiona just came back from the dead! I've been waiting for that for weeks!"

Lee ignored her and sat down in his

41

chair. "It's time for a family meeting on the subject of Warren Cleary. I think this has all gotten way out of hand. Now, I knew Warren personally. I told you before—he was a good guy. He was the one who set up the football pool each year. And he called bingo every Saturday night.

"It was a real tragedy what happened to him. But he's gone. Dead."

Lee shook his head. "Poor Warren. What a terrible thing to happen to such a nice guy."

"Yeah," C.J. said, "but what happened to him was enough to make the nicest guy snap."

CHAPTER 7

Frozen

C.J. had to get out of the house. Now. *He* was going to snap if his family didn't stop talking about Warren Cleary.

He went out back and sat on the bluff. Sunshine filtered through the branches. Two squirrels chased each other overhead. And down below, the slimy creek was still.

Luckily, C.J.'s parents and sister left him alone. He just needed some time to himself.

Was he going crazy? Or was Warren Cleary really after him?

The sun felt so good on his shoulders, C.J. wanted to take a nap. But that really would be crazy! His eyelids closed, but he jerked them back open. They started to close again. Finally he decided to close his eyes, but only for a second.

Suddenly he felt very cold. The sun must have set. Or else clouds had covered it up.

He opened his eyes but couldn't see anything. Had he fallen asleep? Was it already nighttime?

But even if it was nighttime, why was it so cold in the middle of July?

And why did he feel as if he was moving?

Suddenly some lights went on. They were dim and looked very far away, like stars. Except these lights were at eye level instead of in the sky.

It was getting colder by the second.

As C.J.'s eyes adjusted, he saw white smoke swirling around the lights. Then he noticed big brown ice cream containers, the kind his father brought home from the Park's plant. The Bullochs stored them in a big freezer. Was C.J. in some kind of freezer?

Oh, no! Now he realized what was happening. He was in the back of a Park's ice cream truck.

Warren must have grabbed him while he was asleep!

C.J. was freezing. He was having trouble breathing. There wasn't much air in the back of the truck.

He stood up. But the eighteen-wheeler hit a bump and he fell back. His head hit one of the ice cream drums. It was killing him!

C.J. had to escape. But there was just no way. He started to panic. *Finish what you started,* he told himself. *You got thrown in the back of this truck. Now figure out a way to get back out.*

It was lucky his father had just taken him to the truck yard and showed him the insides of one of these monsters. C.J. knew what to find back here. He knew where the refrigeration equipment was. Three strong fans blew out icy air. If he could just smash an ice cream container into the fans, they might break and turn off. Then at least he wouldn't freeze to death.

C.J. rubbed his palms together. He suddenly realized he didn't have any feeling in his ears. What if they froze and broke off? He reached up to massage them. They were covered with frost!

He rubbed off the ice particles. Then he stood up. But he didn't straighten up all the way. If he fell, he didn't want to have to fall very far.

C.J. walked toward the front of the semi-trailer. He tried to keep near the sides of the truck. That was where the lights were, stuck in the floor.

The trouble was that the ice cream containers were piled high against the trailer walls. There was more room in the middle of the trailer, where it was pitch-dark.

Suddenly C.J. tripped over something. He fell flat on his face on top of it. It was as hard as the ice cream containers. But it had a different shape. It was much longer and wider than an ice cream drum. And it felt pointy instead of smooth.

He pushed down hard on the object to hoist himself up.

Whatever it was, it felt bony.

Finally C.J. got his balance and could take a look at what he'd tripped over. It was a person—a kid! Frozen stiff. Frozen as solid as the ice cream in the containers.

C.J. screamed.

He looked around. He saw lots of ice cream containers. And he saw something else—dozens of bodies, all of them frozen. Some of the kids were sitting Indian-style. Four of them were sitting in one another's laps, stacked on the trailer floor. They all had shaggy ice beards.

In one corner a boy was curled up as if he was fast asleep. But C.J. knew he would never wake up.

Another boy was sitting with his hands on his knees. He looked like a human chair!

The truck lurched, and C.J. fell to the icy floor again.

Suddenly it hit him—all these kids were boys about his age!

So the story was true. Warren Cleary was out for revenge. He was looking for the boy who had run out in front of him. Except he couldn't remember what that boy looked like. So he was chasing every boy he saw who was about the right age—just in case one of them happened to be the right one.

And when he caught a kid, he froze him to death.

C.J. knew he had to stop thinking about dying if he wanted to survive. By now he was pretty close to the front of the freezer compartment. He had to get there before he got too cold to move or think. He had to make it in one try.

He stood up and started moving.

He stepped around the bodies, trying not to touch them.

Suddenly the truck slammed to a stop. C.J. hit the floor.

CHAPTER 8

Real Nightmare

When he opened his eyes, C.J. was sitting on the bluff. He felt dizzy. The sun had fallen behind the treetops, but it wasn't dark yet. The crickets were chirping like crazy.

It was that time of day when shadows seemed to move. They looked almost alive.

Unlike Warren Cleary.

One thing C.J. was sure of: He'd had a nightmare. And the bogus tale of the Phantom Trucker was going to keep giving him nightmares—until he got a grip. It was all in his head. He liked scary stories—sometimes. But he had to stop thinking about Warren Cleary. Enough was enough.

If he tried, C.J. figured, he could forget about Warren Cleary by next week.

Until then, C.J. wasn't going to get freaked out. The next time he saw old Warren he was going to show him who was boss.

C.J. was hungry. His mom was making spaghetti tonight, his favorite. It was probably around suppertime. His mom always rang the dinner bell when it was time to eat. He hoped he hadn't missed it while he was sleeping.

C.J. rubbed his eyes and got up to stretch.

Suddenly he saw something move on the other side of the creek.

The world was getting darker by the second. The tree shadows were growing longer.

That must be what C.J. was seeing—a shadow. But that shadow was starting to look a lot like a man!

No, his eyes had to be playing tricks on him.

Oh, no—the figure was crossing the creek now. Water and algae sloshed up onto the cypress knees.

The shadow figure was starting to look an awful lot like Warren Cleary.

No way. C.J.'s thoughts were racing. *He isn't really there. And even if he is, he's just a ghost. What's the worst a ghost can do? Don't let him get to you. Don't let him push you around.*

The sloshing sounds were getting louder. The figure was getting closer.

By the time the figure got to the bottom of the bluff, C.J.'s heart was pounding. He wanted to turn around and run inside. But that would be admitting Warren Cleary was real. C.J. wasn't going to do that. And he wasn't going to admit he was scared, not even to himself.

There was only one problem with not being scared: The guy climbing up the bluff sure looked like Warren—C.J. saw the bloody gash, the red hair curling out from under the Park's cap, the blue bandanna around his neck. As he walked, his thick arms swung from his shoulders like clubs.

C.J. shouted down at him, "I don't

51

believe in you, you jerk!"

But Warren kept coming up the bluff.

"I'm not going anywhere, man!" C.J. shouted. "You're the one who's about to disappear!"

Now Warren was so close C.J. could see him smiling. Suddenly his mouth opened beneath that bloody gash. His teeth were yellow and brown. And out of his gross mouth came a deep, horrible laugh.

It all seemed too real—more real than the dream C.J. had just had. So he turned around and started to run.

Too late! He felt Warren's hand grab his shoulder. There was a horrible pain in his neck. But before C.J. could cry out, Warren's bandanna was covering C.J.'s mouth. Warren tied it tight around C.J.'s head.

C.J. shouted for help, but no one could hear him!

"Care to accompany me on a joyride, son?" Warren asked in a hoarse, scratchy voice.

He grabbed C.J.'s elbow and dragged him through the trees, toward the dirt road. C.J. struggled to escape, but Warren was too strong for him. He squeezed his eyes shut and thought, *There's no place like home. There's no place like home.*

When he finally opened his eyes, a purple sky loomed over him. And Warren was dragging him up the ladder of a Park's eighteen-wheeler!

Warren shoved him into the passenger seat and strapped him in tightly. While he walked around to the driver's side, C.J. yanked at the shoulder belt. He pressed the button on the lap belt. But he couldn't get them off. Warren must have rigged them somehow. He squirmed and twisted, but he could hardly move. He was trapped!

He pulled at the bandanna, but it was tied too tight to remove.

The driver's-side door opened.

Suddenly C.J. heard a little girl's voice.

"No, Mama, it isn't Daddy. He's inside taking a nap. Should we go see who's in that truck?"

It was Lulu! C.J. looked out the rolled-up window. He couldn't see his house from where Warren's rig was parked. But he figured Lulu and his mother were sitting on the front porch.

"No, darling," his mother said. "*Wheel of Fortune*'s about to come on. You run out back and try to find your brother."

"I'm in here!" C.J. wanted to shout. But his voice was muffled by the bandanna.

Then C.J. got an idea. If he pushed the heavy passenger-side door open, Lulu and his mom might hear the noise and come check it out. Just this afternoon, his dad had showed him how the doors opened. The door handle was in a strange place in an eighteen-wheeler. But where?

Do it, he told himself as his right hand slid down the inside of the door. *Now.*

Warren turned on the ignition. His hand reached for the enormous gearshift.

Finally C.J. found the door handle. It was down very low on the door. In one swift move, he pulled it and kicked the door open!

Kidnapped

At that moment the rig roared to life. The dirt road rushed beneath the wheels. C.J.'s head bounced against the back of the seat.

Warren stopped the truck and went around to C.J.'s side. He slammed the door. Then he got back in and pressed a button by his door. C.J. heard a click and knew he was locked in.

"Sorry about that," Warren said. "Guess I forgot to lock up. I wouldn't want you to fall out of the truck or anything. You could hurt yourself that way!"

C.J.'s head felt as if it was going to explode. He looked out the window. Although it was dark, he could see pine trees passing by. *His* forest.

At the corner, Warren reached over and untied C.J.'s gag with one hand. C.J. gasped for air and screamed, "Lulu! Mama!"

Warren turned off the dirt road and onto a two-lane paved one.

"They can't hear you," he said.

The rig turned onto the highway.

"Nope, they can't hear you," Warren repeated with a laugh.

C.J. smelled something disgusting and realized what it was—Warren Cleary's breath. Suddenly the truck swerved to the side of the road! C.J. could feel the weight of the semi-trailer being pulled along behind them. The freezer compartment must be full.

"Keep your eyes on the road!" C.J. shouted.

"Good idea," Warren said, straightening up in his lane. There was a lot of traffic on the road. Ahead of them, taillights blurred into a long red stream. "Appreciate it," he added.

C.J. looked around. There was static on the CB radio. The dashboard glowed with yellow, green, and red lights. His father had told him about all those dials and gauges just this morning. But C.J. was so scared he couldn't remember what any of them were for. From the mirror hung a pair of giant fuzzy dice.

"Hey," Warren said, turning to C.J., "I don't believe we've been properly introduced. I'm Warren Cleary. Pleased to make your acquaintance."

Warren stuck out his right hand. Luckily, he kept his left hand on the wheel.

Warren's hand was covered with bristly red hair and warts. C.J. didn't want to take it. But what choice did he have? Warren's palm was rougher than a cat's tongue.

At that moment C.J. knew he definitely wasn't dreaming. Not this time. This was really happening. Because Warren was *real!*

"Did you say something?" Warren asked.

C.J. didn't think he had. He must have been mumbling to himself. He glared at Warren but didn't answer.

"I said, Did you say something?" A vein on Warren's neck bulged. The gash on his face throbbed, and blood dripped down onto the big steering wheel.

"No, I didn't say anything," C.J. managed to say.

"Something about me being real, was that it?" Warren screamed.

C.J. realized that if he wanted to get out of this truck alive, he was going to have to calm Warren down. "I was just saying that you're a real good driver," he said.

Warren quieted down. C.J. wondered if that ugly face had stopped dripping blood. But he kept his eyes on the road. If he looked at this guy—even out of the corner of his eye—he'd freak. They were racing north. Heading far, far away from home.

"Yep, I was born to drive a big rig," Warren said in a faraway voice. "In the old days I had a nice job, a nice family. Not to mention all the ice cream I could eat."

Warren turned to C.J. and said, "Hey, what's your favorite flavor?"

C.J. couldn't believe what he was hearing. How could he think about ice cream at a time like this? "Rocky road," he said finally.

"Mine too!" Warren said. "Ain't that some coincidence! I never liked strawberry much. Too bad you had to take a bath in it!"

C.J. sneaked a glance at Warren. He was staring straight ahead with a distant expression.

"Yep, everything sure was sweet in those days. Collected a regular paycheck. Even had me a little boat."

"That sounds nice," C.J. said.

"Sure was," Warren said. "Then a little something happened. Nothing much. Just a little accident. Hey, you don't happen to know anything about that, do you?"

"About what?"

"About this!" Warren Cleary took both hands off the wheel and ran them down his face. Then he held out his bloody palms for C.J. to see.

"You killed me!" Warren boomed.

The truck crossed the line that divided the highway into lanes. Cars honked. Other trucks blew their horns.

C.J. gripped the sides of his seat. "Watch where you're going!" he shouted.

Warren grabbed the wheel with his bloody hands. "I knew you were the one!" he said.

Warren Cleary was crazy—and angry! How could C.J. convince him he wasn't the boy who'd run in front of his rig two years before?

Two years before. Wait a minute. How could C.J. be the same boy? That boy would be fourteen by now. And C.J. wasn't even twelve yet!

"Hey, Mr. Cleary," C.J. said when the truck was back in its lane and his heart had stopped pounding.

"Call me Warren." He sounded almost friendly. Not at all deadly.

"Okay, um, Warren," C.J. said, breathing deeply. "I can prove I'm not the same kid who made you have your terrible accident."

"It hurt so bad," Warren said. "I was just trying to get out of your way, you little twerp."

"I know," C.J. said. "But it was a different boy. See, I'm only eleven years old. I was only nine when the accident happened."

Warren squinted at him. "If you weren't

60

the one, how do you know when it happened?"

"Everyone knows, I guess," C.J. said. "But my dad just told me about it last night."

Warren kept his eyes on the road. C.J. didn't know if Warren believed him. He hoped so. He didn't want to think about what the Phantom Trucker might have in store for him!

They crossed the bridge over the Savannah River. The marsh was dark. Now they were in South Carolina. C.J. didn't live that far from the state line. But being in a completely different state made him feel very far from home.

Just then the CB radio crackled.

"Break, channel nineteen." It was his father's voice! Channel nineteen was the truckers' special frequency. "Break, channel nineteen."

"Go ahead, breaker," another voice said.

"Appreciate it," Lee said. "KKN 0712, this is Big Daddy putting out an all-points bulletin on my son, C.J. Bulloch. If anyone's seen him—"

C.J. reached down and grabbed the

microphone. "Daddy, it's me! Warren's got me! We're on I-95 heading—"

Before he could finish, Warren had grabbed the microphone from his hand. Then he ripped the cord out of the transmitter. C.J. hoped his father had heard him. If he had, at least he would know they were on I-95.

Then it hit C.J.: I-95 ran all the way from Florida up to Maine. Great. He hadn't even had time to say which direction they were heading in.

"You, young'un," Warren said, "are turning out to be a lot more trouble than you're worth."

That sounded like a threat. What was Warren going to do with him?

C.J. wasn't going to wait to find out.

He grabbed the fuzzy dice with both hands and ground them into Warren's ugly face.

Warren's hands flew up. The truck veered onto the shoulder of the road.

Suddenly Warren stopped struggling. For a second C.J. thought he had smothered him. Then C.J. heard a muffled sound.

Unbelievable! Warren was laughing behind the fuzzy dice.

Meanwhile, the truck was half on the shoulder and half on the road. On the other side of the shoulder was a swamp. C.J. imagined the leech-infested water filling his lungs.

C.J. let go of the dice. Warren just sat in his seat laughing. The truck was still moving, heading off the road.

"Aren't you going to do something?" C.J. shouted.

"Who, me?" Warren asked. "What do you want me to do, twerp?"

"Grab the wheel!" C.J. cried. "If you don't, we're going to die!"

"You mean, *you're* going to die," Warren said. "I'm already dead." He cackled.

The truck veered off the shoulder. They were headed straight toward the black swamp!

63

CHAPTER 10

Staying Alive

C.J. grabbed the enormous wheel and jerked the truck back onto the road.

Warren leaned back and folded his arms over his chest. "It sure is nice to sit back and be driven for a change," he said.

C.J. could barely reach the wheel. The dashboard jutted out between him and Warren. C.J. gripped the wheel with two hands and turned it as far as he could.

Horns blared.

"You need to straighten up," Warren said calmly.

When Lee took him to the Park's plant this morning, he had forgotten to show C.J. one thing—how to drive one of these babies! C.J. glanced at the dials on the dashboard. He wished he knew what they meant.

The speedometer read 40. Then 30. C.J. didn't know how to get the truck to go any faster.

Another rig pulled alongside. Its driver stuck his fist out at them.

"What do I do?" C.J. asked Warren.

"Maybe this will help," Warren said, shifting the huge gear stick and flooring the accelerator.

C.J. was thrown back against his seat. He almost slammed into the door. He looked over and saw the speedometer needle climbing: 40, 50, 60. But nobody was steering! The truck looked as if it was swallowing up the broken line in the middle of the road. They were driving in both lanes at once!

Warren was laughing.

He doesn't care, C.J. figured. *What's the worst thing that could happen to him? He can't die again!*

"Grab the wheel!" C.J. shouted.

"Why should I?" Warren asked.

"Because if you don't we're going to get killed and probably kill someone else too!"

"Okay, I'll take over," Warren said, "but only if you ask nice. What's the magic word?"

C.J. couldn't believe what he was hearing. "Please!" he screamed.

"That's not it," Warren said. "I'll give you a hint. What's our favorite flavor of ice cream?"

"Rocky road!" C.J. shouted. He didn't care if he sounded like the world's biggest dork.

Warren took the wheel, shifted gears, and steered into the right lane. C.J. calmed down. They drove for a long time without talking. The traffic was thinning out. Outside the window C.J. saw trees and more trees. This forest looked so lonely to him. They passed a cluster of gas stations by the side of the highway. But most of the time the rig seemed to be passing through the middle of nowhere.

Would his folks be able to find him out here—wherever "here" was?

C.J. watched the highway way down below. The windshield curved around to the sides of the truck. The view, even at night, was awesome. It would have been kind of cool to road-trip in a big rig—if a crazed dead goon hadn't been at the wheel!

Warren broke the silence. "You don't talk much, do you?" he asked.

I'd rather jump out of a moving truck than talk to an alien like you, C.J. wanted to say. But he didn't want to make Warren mad. So he just said, "I guess not."

"That's too bad," Warren said. "I thought you were a talker."

C.J. didn't respond.

"Because if you're not going to keep me company," Warren went on, "I might as well just put you back there right now." He gestured over his shoulder toward the trailer behind them.

C.J. swallowed hard. His dream came back to him—if it *was* a dream. He was about to be frozen alive!

Then something occurred to him. C.J. was going to have to talk Warren out of throwing him into the deep freeze. The longer C.J. stayed in the front seat, the more chances he'd have to escape. But once Warren threw him in the back, he was a goner, like the rest of the boys back there!

So C.J. said, "Do you think the Braves will go all the way again this year?"

"I stopped following baseball a couple of years ago," Warren answered.

Probably about the same time you stopped brushing your teeth, C.J. figured.

"I got more important things to worry about now," Warren said.

For the next few miles C.J. couldn't think of anything to say. But he knew he had to come up with something if he didn't want to end up like those frozen kids.

"My dad told me he knew you," C.J. said finally. Just then he felt so homesick, he wanted to cry. But he knew he had to be strong, or he'd never get out of this truck in one piece.

"Yeah, I knew him," Warren replied. "So what?"

"Nothing," C.J. said. "It's just that he said you were a nice guy."

"He did?" Warren turned to C.J. and smiled, showing his mouthful of rotten teeth.

"Yeah," C.J. said, forcing himself to look at Warren's horrible face. He felt as if he was going to throw up.

"Well, I never did like to say a mean word about nobody."

"That's what I heard," C.J. said. This strategy seemed to be working. "Dad said you liked football."

"That's right. The Falcons aren't so hot, I'll give you that. But you've got to support your home team."

The Falcons were so bad that even Georgians didn't like them. But C.J. wasn't about to argue at a time like this.

"Yeah," C.J. said, "go Falcons!"

Warren started talking about the time the Falcons won a game or something. C.J. got busy thinking. He had bought himself some time. Now he had to figure a way out.

Just then, Warren pulled into the left lane. He was passing another truck. C.J. got an idea. He would roll down the window and shout something at the other driver.

C.J. reached for the window crank. Maybe the other driver had heard his father's all-points bulletin on the CB radio.

C.J.'s fingers moved across the truck door. But he couldn't find the crank. And then he realized why. All that remained was a sharp metal stump. Warren had ripped the crank off!

CHAPTER
11

Running on Empty

Warren was still talking.

C.J. pressed his face to the window. "Help!" he mouthed silently.

The other driver looked back. He had sideburns shaped like pork chops, and a V-neck T-shirt. His mouth hung open.

"Help!" C.J. silently called out again. By now Warren's rig had almost passed the other one.

The other driver started smiling and waving. What a dork!

"Then in eighty-three they had a really great year," Warren was saying. "Remember Steve Bartkowski?"

"Uh-huh," C.J. said. He wanted Warren to think he was paying attention. Like he really cared what had happened in 1983, back in the Ice Age. Especially when he was about to be turned into ice himself!

A sign reading WELCOME TO MANNING flashed past them.

C.J. glanced over at the speedometer. Warren was going 65 miles an hour. Then 70. The signs C.J. had seen from the window read SPEED LIMIT—65.

C.J. figured once you were dead, you didn't have to obey traffic rules. But weren't there any police around to catch Warren?

The red lights of a semi-trailer appeared in front of them. Warren started pulling around it.

C.J. tried to get this driver's attention. His lips were almost pressed against the glass.

The other driver saw C.J. and looked at him with a puzzled expression.

"Don't you agree?" Warren was asking.

C.J. didn't know what he was talking about. And he didn't have any time to waste trying to figure it out.

The other driver sped up. Now their trucks were moving at the same speed.

"Hey, what's that guy doing?" Warren asked. "Can't he see I'm trying to pass him?"

Their speed rose to 80 miles an hour. The other driver kept up. He was looking at C.J., trying to figure out what he was saying.

"Help me!" C.J. mouthed as carefully as he could.

Suddenly he felt a hand on his shoulder. He turned around. Warren was furious.

"What do you think you're doing?" he growled.

"Nothing!" C.J. said.

Warren shifted gears and pressed down on the accelerator. The speedometer showed 90 miles an hour.

"It didn't look like nothing to me!" Warren said. His face spurted fresh blood.

C.J.'s heart pounded, but he knew he had to keep calm if he wanted to stay alive. "Hey, did you know my father's a big

73

Falcons fan?" he said.

"Shut up!" Warren shouted, pulling in front of the other rig. "I've had enough of your mouth."

"But I thought you wanted me to keep you company," C.J. croaked.

"I'm tired of your company," Warren said.

"We could listen to the radio," C.J. suggested.

The truck slowed down.

"You're not really going to put me back there, are you?" C.J. pleaded.

"You're going to get what's coming to you," Warren said.

The speedometer needle dropped to 50, then 40.

"I think it's time," Warren said.

The dark woods thinned out. C.J. saw a sign: EXIT 43. ^{1}/$_2$ MILE. FOOD. GAS.

A yellow fluorescent sign flashed high above them on a long pole. The sign read MA'S TRUCK STOP.

Warren turned off the highway.

Just reading the words "Ma's Truck Stop" made C.J. shiver. This was the place where some other truckers had told his father they'd seen Warren Cleary on the road. And it was where Warren had had his horrible accident!

"Yep, I think the time has come," Warren said, turning to C.J. as he hit the brakes.

Time for what? C.J. wanted to know. He pictured those frozen boys he'd stumbled over in his dream. Their ice beards and frost-covered faces were impossible to forget. They pulled into Ma's parking lot. Warren found a space at the end of a row of eighteen-wheelers. The space was right by the woods.

Warren came around to C.J.'s side and pulled open the door.

It was time for C.J. to be frozen—alive!

CHAPTER 12

Truck Stop

"Yep," Warren said, looking down at his watch, "I think it's time—for a nice strong cup of coffee. I'm hungry, too. I sure would enjoy a slice of pie. A la mode!" He winked at C.J.

C.J. heaved a sigh of relief. So he wasn't going to be thrown in the deep freeze—at least not yet. But his heart was still pounding. Ma's Truck Stop would probably be his last chance to escape. He had to think of a plan. If he blew it, he was going to be a

Popsicle by tomorrow!

Warren had pulled his cap brim all the way down. He almost looked like a normal human being now.

He started to undo C.J.'s safety belts. Then he stopped. "Now, you just walk a little in front of me, and we'll both be fine. But here's some advice. If you try to run, you won't win. Did I mention I finished the Peachtree Marathon?"

"Great," C.J. mumbled.

"Oh, and one other thing," Warren said. "Keep your mouth shut. One word and you're the flavor of the month."

C.J. rolled his eyes.

"Are you as hungry as I am?" Warren asked as he finished undoing C.J.'s safety belts. "Or would you rather wait in the back?"

"Yeah, I'm starving," C.J. said sarcastically. But, come to think of it, he *was* pretty hungry.

They walked slowly to the restaurant. Warren's huge meaty hand was clamped around C.J.'s upper arm. The building had big windows. From the parking lot you could see how it glowed with a warm yellow light. The place looked crowded.

C.J. and Warren walked in under a sign that read PROFESSIONAL DRIVERS ONLY. They sat down at the counter. The restaurant smelled of grease.

A woman in a waitress uniform came out of the kitchen. She had pink hair under a hairnet. It looked as if she had a giant bag of cotton candy on her head. Her name tag read VESTRA.

"How are y'all tonight?" she asked, handing them two big stiff menus. Then she turned Warren's coffee cup over and filled it.

"Can't complain, miss," Warren said, looking down at his menu.

I can! C.J. wanted to say.

"Well, that's nice to hear," Vestra said. "Seems like every time you turn on the TV, there's somebody complaining about this and that. But I expect you don't get much time to watch those talk shows."

Warren lifted his head slightly but didn't say anything.

C.J. almost jumped in. Then he remembered Warren's threat and kept quiet.

"This your son?" Vestra asked.

"You could say that," Warren said, sipping his coffee.

C.J. got an idea. Warren had told him not to talk. That didn't mean he had to sit still! While Warren read his menu, C.J. looked at Vestra and winked in Warren's direction. Then C.J. made the most hideous face he could. He curled his lips back and made his teeth into fangs and scrunched up his nose and rolled his eyes around. Then he opened his mouth and breathed out, like a fire-breathing dragon.

Vestra smiled at him and went to the other end of the counter.

Over the loudspeaker came a man's deep voice: "Tammy, driver for Dixie Crystals, you have a call on line two!"

"They used to call my name like that," Warren said, stirring his coffee. "My beautiful wife, Glendora, couldn't stand it when I was away. She had me paged wherever I went."

"I need to use the bathroom," C.J. said.

"Later," Warren said. "And keep quiet. That waitress is coming back."

Vestra appeared in front of them. "Now what can I get y'all?"

C.J. started making faces again. Warren was looking down at his menu. C.J. made eye contact with Vestra and pointed at Warren.

"I'll just have a piece of your lemon meringue pie," Warren said.

Vestra looked as if she wasn't paying attention to Warren. As if she had her mind on something else. Was C.J. finally getting through to her? She squinted at Warren and put down her pen. Then she reached into her uniform pocket and took out sparkly cat's-eye glasses. She put them on and stared at Warren.

Yes! C.J. thought. *She recognizes him!*

"I thought I recognized that cap," Vestra said. "Park's ice cream! Why, that's what we serve here at Ma's. I couldn't read the lettering without my glasses."

Great, C.J. thought. *A waitress with bad eyesight.* She probably couldn't even see the faces he was making!

"I'm going to bring you some Park's ice cream with that pie," Vestra announced.

"On the house. What about you, son? Would you care for some pie and ice cream too?"

"Sure, he'd love it," Warren said.

Vestra looked at C.J. with a sad smile. "You'll get over being shy someday," she said. "Believe it or not, I was shy as a girl myself. Now look at me!"

Then she went back into the kitchen.

The last thing in the world C.J. wanted to eat was Park's ice cream.

He was starting to feel desperate. He considered running up to some stranger in a booth. But what would he say? "Uh, sir, I've been kidnapped by a ghost trucker. He's sitting right over there at the counter. Would you please call the police?"

They'd all think *he* was the crazy one.

And Warren would be madder than ever.

"I saw what you were doing," Warren whispered out of the corner of his mouth.

C.J. froze with fear.

"Don't think I didn't. But if you eat up when your pie comes, I'll let you ride up front with me a while longer."

C.J. didn't believe that for a second. As soon as they finished eating, C.J. was a

81

goner. He had to escape. And he had to do it now!

He had to get people to notice him. But no one would believe him…unless they saw for themselves. If C.J. pulled Warren's cap off, if they saw his scary face…

C.J. swiveled on his stool and swung his hand up to Warren's cap.

He clamped his fingers tightly around the brim.

But before he could pull the cap off, Warren was gripping his wrist. C.J. couldn't move his arm!

"All right, young'un, I've had it with you," Warren said. He pulled C.J. off the stool. "I guess you're just going to have to have your ice cream in the truck. Well, there's plenty of it back there." He started dragging C.J. through the restaurant.

"Help!" C.J. cried. "It's Warren Cleary, everybody! He's a ghost and he's got me!"

A couple of people laughed. But nobody did anything. As if they saw a guy dragging a kid through Ma's Truck Stop every day! What was wrong with them? Fathers didn't bring their kids to places like this!

Outside, Warren held C.J. with one hand

and opened the back of the trailer with the other. "Yep, there's lots of ice cream back here. But I don't know if there's a spoon. Sorry about that. Oh—and make sure you don't mistake some kid for a container of chocolate chip."

The metal trailer door rolled up. Freezing air blew out at them. Warren picked C.J. up and threw him in.

CHAPTER 13

Knockout!

C.J. landed flat on his stomach. He could feel icy steel against his cheek and under his fingertips. If he didn't act fast, his skin would soon be stuck to the trailer floor.

In a split second he was up. Warren was reaching for the door handle. C.J. grabbed a container of ice cream. As the door slid down, C.J. threw the drum at Warren. It smashed him right in the face!

Warren fell backward. C.J. scrambled out of the truck.

Warren lay on his back against the parking lot. His cap had flown off his head. Blood spread all over his face.

Warren seemed to be out cold, but C.J. wasn't taking any chances.

He tried to hoist Warren up. He stuck his hands under Warren's arms and pulled and pulled. Sweat stung C.J.'s eyes. Finally, he got the top part of Warren's body into the truck. Then he grabbed Warren's boots. In one movement C.J. flipped him over. Warren Cleary's body back-flipped into the freezer compartment.

C.J. couldn't believe what he'd done. But he had no time to waste standing around feeling proud of himself. He pulled the semi-trailer's door down. Then he ran into the restaurant.

"Help!" he shouted. "Help!"

C.J. spotted Vestra at the counter. He ran up to her.

"You can talk!" Vestra exclaimed. "What happened to your daddy?"

"He's not my daddy!" C.J. said. "He's Warren Cleary, the Phantom Trucker! And I just threw him in the back of his rig, ma'am.

85

He might be dead—but he might not be!"

Vestra shook her head. "I see your daddy's been telling you those same trashy stories I have to listen to all day long." She wiped a spot on the counter. "Now, where's he at? He's going to have to pay for that pie, even if I did have to throw it out. It's a sin to waste perfectly good food."

C.J. could see he wasn't getting anywhere with Vestra. So he turned to a man in a cowboy hat, who was sitting at the counter. "Please, mister," C.J. said, "can you give me a hand out in the parking lot?"

"I heard what you said about old Warren Cleary," the cowboy trucker said, laughing. "But I reckon I don't believe in ghosts."

"Well, this is one awfully heavy ghost!" C.J. said. "I picked him up myself."

The cowboy trucker looked him up and down. "A young feller like you picked up Warren Cleary all by himself?"

"Well, I kind of flipped him over. He's in the back of the rig now. But I don't know how to lock the door. I need to lock it before he wakes up—if he wakes up!"

The cowboy gulped his coffee. "Okay,"

he said. "Let's put the pedal to the metal."

They went out into the hot night. C.J. looked across the parking lot. Warren's rig was gone!

"Where to, pardner?" the cowboy trucker asked.

"It's...it's gone!" C.J. said. "It was just here a minute ago. I swear it was!"

The cowboy trucker just looked at C.J. and shook his head. "I need to get back to that cup of coffee before it gets cold."

"Wait," C.J. said. "At least let me use your radio to call my dad. He's probably out looking for me."

"Well..." the cowboy said.

"Rocky road!" C.J. burst out.

"How's that?" the cowboy asked, looking puzzled.

"I mean, please!" C.J. cried. He couldn't believe it—Warren had really gotten to him! *Don't lose it now,* he told himself.

"All right," the cowboy said. "My rig's just over there. I guess it couldn't hurt."

"Thanks," C.J. said.

They walked over to the cowboy's rig. C.J. was relieved to see there weren't any ice cream cones painted on the trailer.

The cowboy opened the door and clicked on a knob. The CB radio crackled to life. The cowboy jumped down and C.J. hopped in.

C.J. sat in the driver's seat and picked up the microphone. "KKN 0712, base to mobile—I mean, mobile to mobile—come in, Big Daddy, come in, Big Daddy."

Down below, the cowboy trucker was whistling a sad tune.

"This is Big Daddy," Lee Bulloch's voice boomed from the receiver. "That you, Little Darling?"

"Ten-four, Big Daddy!"

"Boy, am I glad to hear your voice, son! Your mama and I have been worried sick. Are you all right? Where are you?"

"I'm fine, Dad. I'm at Ma's Truck Stop. You know where that is, right?"

"Ten-four. Stay right inside the restaurant. I'm just a few miles south of there. Big Daddy, over and out."

What a relief! If C.J. could just stay out of Warren Cleary's clutches for the next few minutes, things would work out okay.

Just then a woman's voice came on the CB. "Break, channel nineteen. Break, channel nineteen."

"Go ahead, breaker," a man's voice replied.

"I appreciate it. This is Tornado Tanya calling Cowboy Carl. Come in, Cowboy Carl."

"Hey, that's me!" the cowboy trucker said. "Get on down from there and let me up. That's my old lady calling."

"Thanks a lot, Cowboy Carl," C.J. said, jumping down.

"No problem, kid."

C.J. headed back across the parking lot. He couldn't wait to see his father. And his mom. He wouldn't even mind seeing Lulu right now.

Just then he heard a roaring sound getting louder and louder.

Warren Cleary's rig was heading straight at him!

89

CHAPTER 14

Crash!

C.J. froze. Warren's rig was getting closer. With its bright yellow headlights, the truck looked like a ten-ton steel-and-chrome tiger bearing down on him.

In front of C.J. was another row of eighteen-wheelers. There was no way around them.

So C.J. shot off to his left, between two rows of trucks. Warren's rig was gaining on him. Its roar was getting louder and louder.

There was a patch of woods at the end

of the parking lot. If C.J. could just get to the woods, he'd have a chance.

But the trees were too far away. And Warren's rig was too close. C.J. was never going to make it! His lungs were about to collapse. How could he outrun an eighteen-wheeler?

He was about to be flattened against the pavement. What a way to die! C.J. almost wished Warren had just thrown him in the deep freeze from the start. At least then he could have closed his eyes and gone to sleep…

Finish what you started, said a voice inside C.J.'s head. *If you're going to try to escape, then go for it!*

He pushed on as hard as he could. The trees were getting closer.

At the edge of the parking lot a streetlight cast a white circle onto the asphalt. With a final burst of energy C.J. crossed into the white circle, like a runner crossing a finish line.

His lungs filled with smoke from the truck's two smokestacks. He could feel the truck's hot metal breath against his back.

C.J. threw himself into the trees and collapsed. Warren was going too fast to stop.

His rig crashed into the light pole. The light exploded, sending off sparks. C.J. saw Warren cover his face. But the pole smashed into the windshield, right where Warren was sitting.

The rig was slowing down. Would it stop before hitting C.J.? He was too exhausted to move, but the truck was heading straight for him!

The truck struck a pine tree and knocked it down. Then it hit a second pine tree and came to a stop—just inches from C.J.!

He lay there for a few seconds, coughing and trying to catch his breath. Then he forced himself to get up. His legs felt as heavy as blocks of ice. He could barely stumble out of the woods.

People were streaming out of the restaurant. Cowboy Carl jumped out of his rig. "Hey, young feller," he said, putting his arm around C.J. "Are you okay?"

C.J. gulped air. "I'm all right."

"Who was driving that rig?" Cowboy Carl whispered to C.J. "It wasn't that ghost trucker you were talking about, was it?"

"See for yourself," C.J. said.

Other truckers were coming up to C.J. Still others ran over to the ruined truck.

Vestra came out with a bowl of ice cream. "You poor thing!" she said. "Here, eat this, it'll give you some strength!"

C.J. couldn't believe his eyes. Rocky road. This was *not* his day. "May I just have some ice water, ma'am?" he asked.

"You bet!" Vestra said, running back inside.

Sirens blared. Then two fire trucks and three police cars pulled in to the lot.

Suddenly C.J. heard a familiar voice.

"Daddy, he's over here!"

C.J. turned, and there was Lulu! His father was right behind her.

Lulu reached up and gave him a hug. "We thought Warren got you for sure!" she said.

"He almost did," said C.J. "Hey, what are you doing here anyway?"

"Daddy needed me to ride with him to identify the vehicle. I told Mama there was something fishy about that truck in our yard!"

Better late than never, C.J. figured.

"Mama's home listening to the CB," Lulu went on. "Some other truckers saw you on the road. That's how we knew what direction to go in."

"Son," his father said, slapping C.J. on the back, "it sure is good to see you!"

"Ditto," C.J. said.

"Is Warren gone for good?" asked Lulu.

"He must be," C.J. replied, looking across the lot at the crashed truck at the edge of the woods. Firemen were hosing down the wreckage.

While Lulu was rattling on about something, a policeman left the wreck and came up to C.J. "Are you the boy who was involved in that accident?" he asked.

"Yes, sir, I was," C.J. answered.

"Did you get hurt?"

"I think I'm okay," C.J. said.

"Good," said the officer. "I just need to ask you a couple of questions. First of all, can you tell me who was driving the vehicle?"

"Yes, sir," C.J. said. "It was Warren Cleary."

The officer wrote down the name. "Can you describe him for me?"

C.J. wondered why the policeman wanted a description. Couldn't he see that goon for himself?

A grim thought popped into C.J.'s head. Maybe Warren was looking so hideous after the crash that they couldn't identify his body.

"Is he dead?" C.J. asked. As soon as he'd said it, he wondered, *Can a dead man die again?*

"We don't know," the officer said. "We'll have to find him, or his body, before we can determine that."

"Find his body?" Lulu asked in a trembling voice.

C.J.'s father put one hand on Lulu's shoulder and the other on C.J.'s.

"Yeah," the officer said. "When we got to the scene of the accident, the cab was empty. The driver was gone."

The police officer asked C.J. some more questions. Then C.J., Lulu, and their father headed back to the Bullochs' pickup truck.

The three of them walked without saying anything. C.J. looked around. Most of the truckers had gone back inside. Vestra had given him his glass of water and waited for him to drink it. Then she'd taken the glass, pecked him on the cheek, and gone back inside, too.

Blue and red lights lit up Warren Cleary's rig. It was still right where he'd crashed it.

The back of the semi-trailer was open. As they walked past Warren's rig, C.J. stopped and looked inside. All he could see in the freezer compartment were stacks of ice cream containers.

No dead bodies, no Warren Cleary. Could C.J. have imagined the whole thing? No way. He'd almost gotten killed! Besides, *someone* had to have wrecked that truck.

A policeman told C.J. to move along. As he walked to the pickup truck, something occurred to him. Warren Cleary had just had the same accident that had killed him two years ago. C.J. thought about his dad's story: Warren crashed into a light pole at the edge of Ma's parking lot. His windshield was smashed. His face got cut in two.

And this time it was C.J.'s fault.

Had Warren Cleary really died this time?

C.J. sure hoped so. Because if Warren Cleary was still out there somewhere, he was going to be angrier than ever at C.J.— and every other kid he came across on the road.

"You doing okay?" Lee asked, putting his arm around his son's shoulders.

"Yeah, Dad," C.J. said. It felt great to be with his family again. "I'm doing just fine."

"Yeah," Lulu said, "he's back to his weird old self."

"I'm feeling too good to be mad, even at you, Lulu," C.J. said.

The second they got in the pickup truck, Rhonda's voice came across the CB. She didn't bother to ask for air clearance or use the Bullochs' call numbers. "Did you get him, Big Daddy?" she asked. "Is he okay?"

"Ten-four, Big Mama," Lee said.

"Oh, that's wonderful!" Rhonda said. "Because I didn't know how much longer I could sit here by the radio. I'm getting faint from hunger!"

C.J. laughed. Nothing had changed back home.

"How about picking us up some ribs at Sweet 'n' Smoky's?" his mom asked.

C.J. picked up the microphone. "You got it, Big Mama."

"That's my boy!" she said. "This is Big Mama, over and out."

As they pulled out of the parking lot, C.J. turned around and took one last look at the wrecked rig in the dark woods.

No sign of Warren—for now.

Jason K. Friedman was born in Savannah, Georgia, and has also written a book about haunted houses. He lives in Seattle, Washington, with his best friend, in an old apartment building overlooking the highway. He has eaten at truck stops across the country.

Take a bite out of something fang-tastic!

CAROL ELLIS

VAMPIRE CATS

I couldn't believe my sister was actually going through with it. How could she *marry* Creep-o-Kurt?

My bridesmaid's dress itched like crazy. To take my mind off it, I checked out the food table. A black cat was creeping among the platters. Blackjack!

Leaping from the table, he landed silently on the grass. Belly low to the ground, eyes narrowed to slits, he began slinking across the yard toward the wedding party.

The minister took a deep breath. "Dearly beloved…"

Suddenly, Blackjack launched himself off the ground. Claws out, ears back, teeth bared, he soared through the air like a rocket. Snarling and spitting, the cat landed on Kurt's shoulder.

"Yaahh!" Kurt howled. He grabbed Blackjack's tail and yanked—hard.

My sister screamed. The guests gasped.

And Blackjack sank his fangs deep into Kurt's neck…

Sink your teeth into something fun!

CAROL ELLIS

You can find FANGS titles wherever books are sold...

OR

You can send in this coupon (with check or money order)
and have the books mailed directly to you!

- -

❑ **#1   VAMPIRE CATS (0-679-88162-X) $3.99**

Tiffany is heartbroken when her best friend, Richie, moves away. But things start to look up when she adopts a mysterious stray black cat. Tiffany's new pet arrives just in time to ruin her big sister's wedding—and turn it into a screaming vampire cat fight!

❑ **#2   OVERNIGHT BITE (0-679-88163-8) $3.99**

What boy doesn't wonder what girls talk about behind closed doors? Damian, an extremely cute vampire boy, invites himself to Ginger's super-secret slumber party. Disguised as a bat, he flaps around in her attic, until Ginger leaves her guests to investigate. Big mistake!

Subtotal . . . . $ _____

Shipping and handling . . . . $ __3.00__

Sales tax (where applicable). . . . . $ _____

Total amount enclosed. $ _____

Name _____

Address _____

City _____ **State** ____ **Zip** _____

Make your check or money order (no cash or C.O.D.s) payable to Random House
and mail to: Bullseye Mail Sales, 400 Hahn Road, Westminster, MD 21157.

Prices and numbers subject to change without notice. Valid in U.S. only.
All orders subject to availability. Please allow 4 to 6 weeks for delivery.

**Need your books even faster? Call toll-free 1-800-793-2665
to order by phone and use your major credit card.
Please mention interest code 049-20 to expedite your order.**

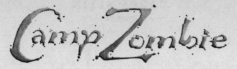

Gooflumps

WARNING! NOT A GOOSE-BUMPS BOOK

THIS SPOOF IS JUST A GOOF!

by R.U. Slime

You can find GOOFLUMPS titles wherever books are sold...

OR

*You can send in this coupon (with check or money order)
and have the books mailed directly to you!*

❑ **#2½ STAY OUT OF THE BATHROOM** $3.99
(0-679-87908-0)

Joe is a terror on the toilet! He won't put down the seat. Not now. Not ever. But the bully of the bowl has met his match. It's payback time—and The Toilet is plunging into action!

❑ **#4½ EAT CHEESE AND BARF!** $3.99
(0-679-87935-8)

Chunks city! Billy Fudder is a dairy dork—a hurling horror— when it comes to milk products. Too bad his new town is dairy capital of the world! Billy and his new friend, Fanny, discover a cheese brain in the basement—a slimy cottage cheese mon- ster! Barf-o-rama!

AN UNAUTHORIZED PARODY

Subtotal . . . . $ _____
Shipping and handling . . . . $ ___3.00___
Sales tax (where applicable) . . . $ _____
Total amount enclosed . . . . $ _____

Name_____

Address_____

City _____State _____Zip _____

Make your check or money order (no cash or C.O.D.s) payable to Random House
and mail to: Bullseye Mail Sales, 400 Hahn Road, Westminster, MD 21157.

Prices and numbers subject to change without notice. Valid in U.S. only.
All orders subject to availability. Please allow 4 to 6 weeks for delivery.

Need your books even faster? Call toll-free 1-800-793-2665
to order by phone and use your major credit card.
Please mention interest code 049-20 to expedite your order.